W9-CGT-478

Generous Me

WRITTEN BY MARY E. PEARSON
ILLUSTRATED BY GARY KREJCA

Children's Press®
A Division of Scholastic Inc.
New York • Toronto • London • Auckland • Sydney
Mexico City • New Delhi • Hong Kong
Danbury, Connecticut

For Susan, who really did share with
her whining little sister
—M.E.P.

To my nieces: Candace, Jordan, and Makayla
—G.K.

Reading Consultant

Katharine A. Kane
Education Consultant
(Retired, San Diego County Office of Education and
San Diego State University)

Library of Congress Cataloging-in-Publication Data

Pearson, Mary (Mary E.)
  Generous me / written by Mary E. Pearson ; illustrated by Gary Krejca.
       p. cm.—(Rookie reader)
  Summary: An older sister lists all the things she would willingly share with her younger sister, such as her
broccoli and her chores.
  ISBN 0-516-22253-8 (lib. bdg.)   0-516-27819-3 (pbk.)
  [1. Sharing—Fiction. 2. Sisters—Fiction. 3. Humorous stories. 4. Stories in rhyme.] I. Krejca, Gary, ill. II. Title.
III. Series.
  PZ8.3.P27472 Ge 2002
  [E]— dc21
                              2001008347

CHILDREN'S PRESS, AND A ROOKIE READER®, and all associated logos
are trademarks and or registered trademarks of Grolier Publishing Co., Inc.
SCHOLASTIC and associated logos are trademarks and or registered trademarks
of Scholastic Inc.
1 2 3 4 5 6 7 8 9 10 R 11 10 09 08 07 06 05 04 03 02

My sister whines and whines.
She says it isn't fair.

She tattles to my mom
that I refuse to share.

There are lots of things
that I would give her—all for free!
Things that she could *have*
if she wouldn't bother me!

I would give her my broccoli,

my carrots, my sprouts,

Mom's wet mushy kisses,

and all my time-outs.

15

The warts on my elbow,

my homework,

my chores,

and when I'm grounded,
the staying indoors.

My broken night-light,

the scab on my chin,

my wet slimy slugs
in their old rusty tin.

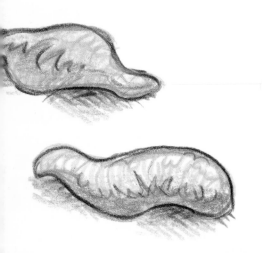

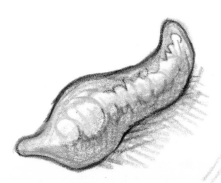

She says I won't share?
It just isn't true!

Why only last week,
I gave her the flu!

Word List (73 words)

all	have	night-light	their
and	her	of	there
are	homework	old	things
bother	I	on	time-outs
broccoli	I'm	only	tin
broken	if	refuse	to
carrots	in	rusty	true
chin	indoors	says	warts
chores	isn't	scab	week
could	it	share	wet
elbow	just	she	when
fair	kisses	sister	whines
flu	last	slimy	why
for	lots	slugs	won't
free	me	sprouts	would
gave	mom	staying	wouldn't
generous	Mom's	tattles	
give	mushy	that	
grounded	my	the	

About the Author

Mary E. Pearson is a writer and teacher in San Diego, Californ

About the Illustrator

Gary Krejca lives in Phoenix, Arizona, with his
wife Kim, their two dogs Chester and Jocko, and
their cat Nick.